istvan banyai

the other side

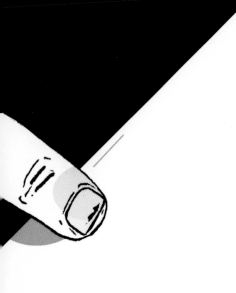

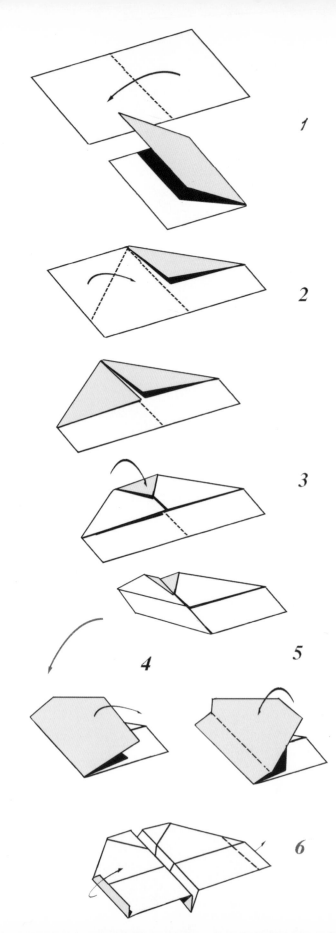

1

2

3

5

4

6

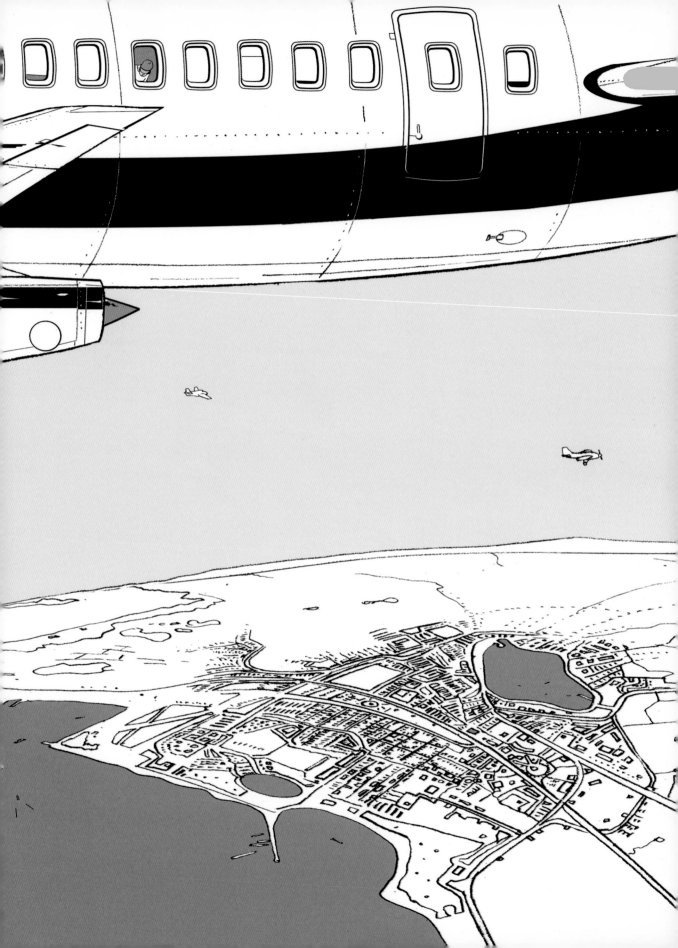

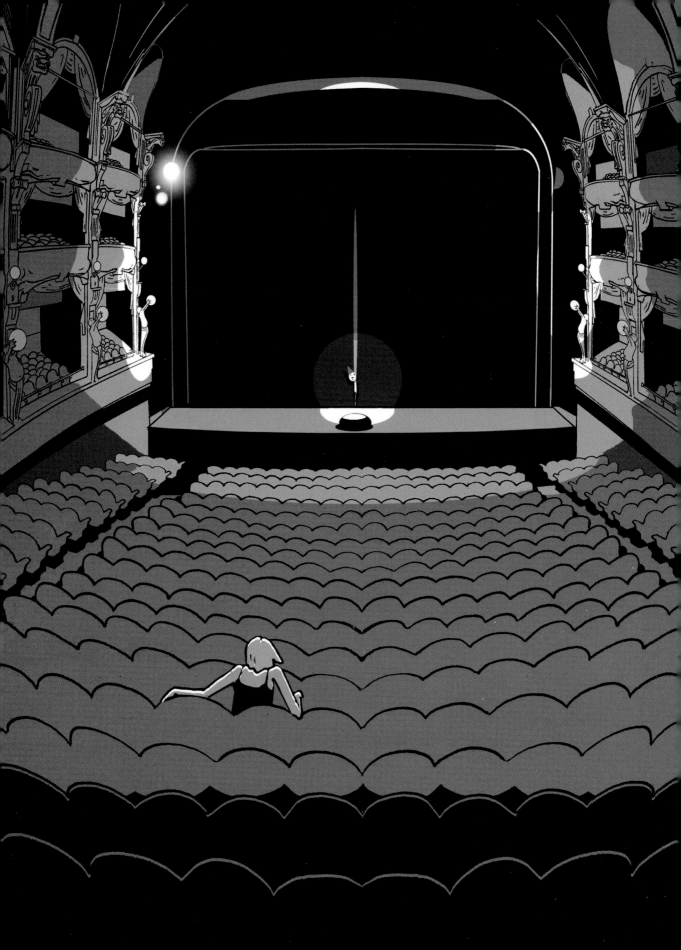

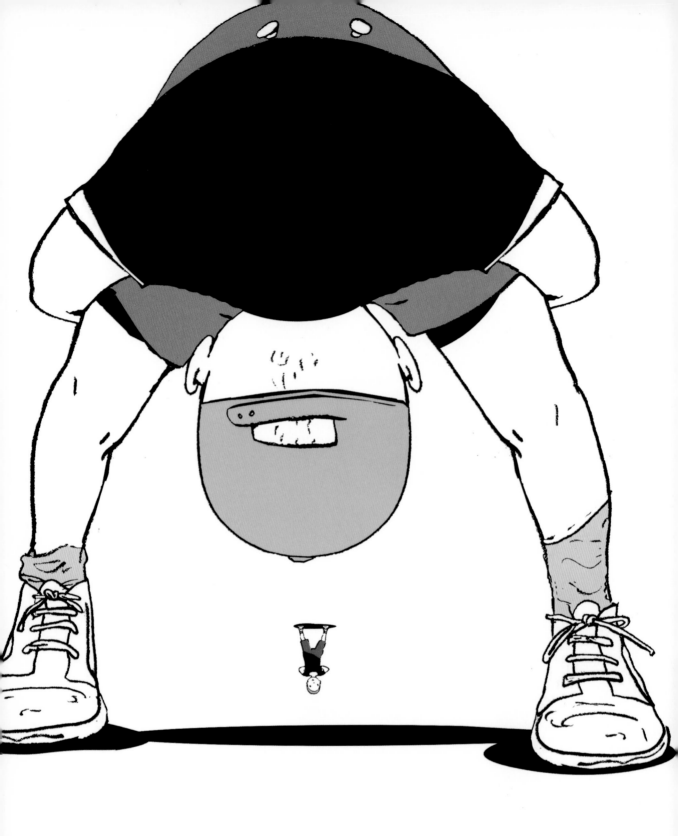

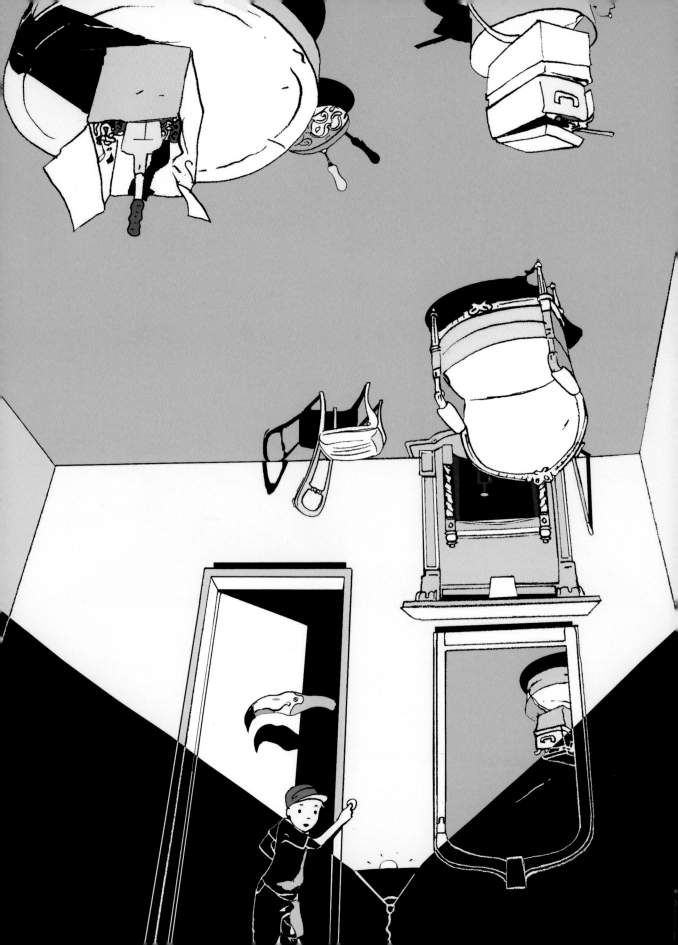

LOOP

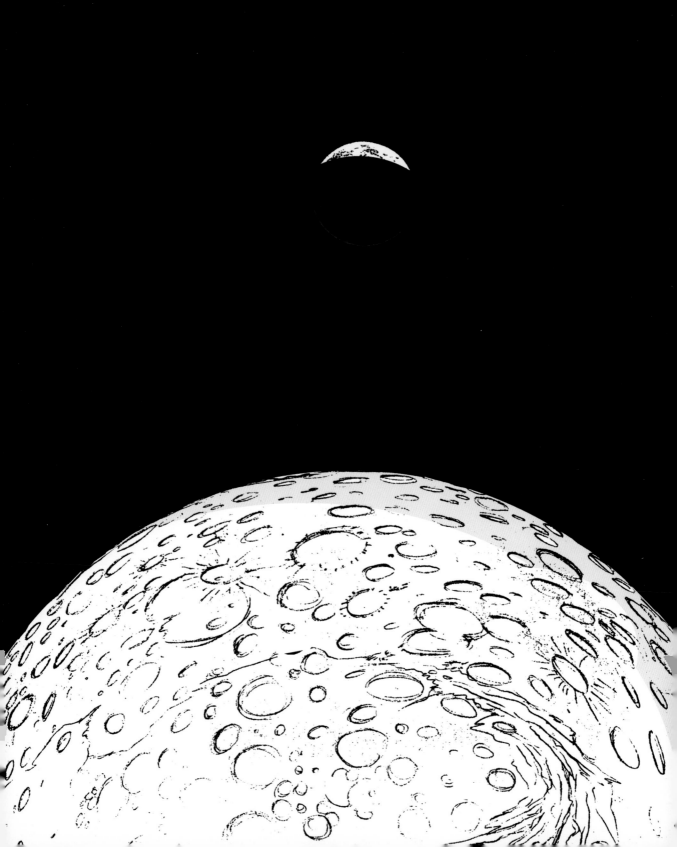

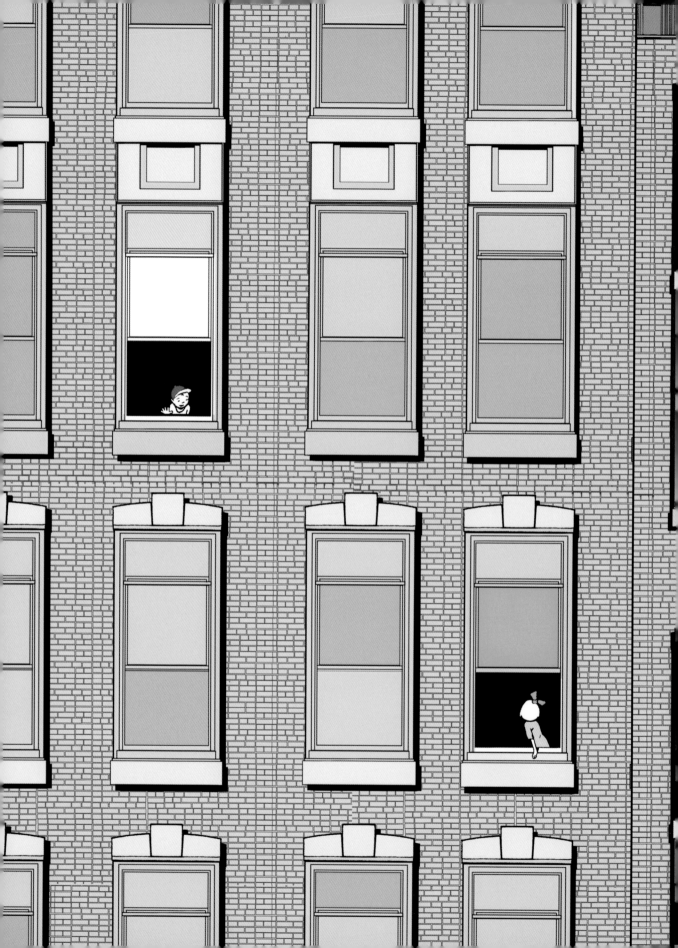

for dora

Book design by Istvan Banyai and Sara Gillingham.
Typeset in Reinert Upright and Hoefler Didot.
The illustrations in this book were rendered in graphite
and colored digitally.
Manufactured in China.

Library of Congress Cataloging-in-Publication Data
Banyai, Istvan.
The other side / by Istvan Banyai.
p. cm.
Summary: A wordless picture book that shows a series
of familiar scenes through many twists in point of view,
such as a boy looking down out of a jet's window and
another boy on the ground looking up at the same jet.
ISBN 0-8118-4608-3
[1. Visual perception—Fiction. 2. Stories without words.]
I. Title.
 PZ7.B22947Ot 2005
[E]—dc22
2004063448

Distributed in Canada by Raincoast Books
9050 Shaughnessy Street, Vancouver, British Columbia
V6P 6E5

10 9 8 7 6 5 4 3 2 1

Chronicle Books LLC
85 Second Street, San Francisco, California 94105

www.chroniclekids.com

chronicle books · san francisco